Sports Illustrated KIDS

Who Wants to Play Just for Kicks?

by Chris Kreie
illustrated by Jorge Santillan

STONE ARCH BOOKS
a capstone imprint

Sports Illustrated KIDS *Who Wants to Play Just for Kicks?*
is published by Stone Arch Books — A Capstone Imprint
151 Good Counsel Drive, P.O. Box 669
Mankato, Minnesota 56002
www.capstonepub.com

Art Director and Designer: Bob Lentz
Creative Director: Heather Kindseth
Production Specialist: Michelle Biedscheid

Timeline photo credits: Shutterstock/Perry Correll (top
left); Sports Illustrated/Jerry Cooke (top right), Peter Read
Miller (middle left & bottom left), Simon Bruty (middle
right & bottom right).

Library of Congress Cataloging-in-Publication Data is
available on the Library of Congress website.

ISBN: 978-1-4342-2229-9 (library binding)
ISBN: 978-1-4342-3079-9 (paperback)

Summary: Josh does not want to take time away from hockey
to play soccer for fun.

Printed in the United States of America in Stevens Point, Wisconsin.
092010   005934WZS11

TABLE of CONTENTS

CHAPTER 1
Spring Break **6**

CHAPTER 2
No Fun at All. **14**

CHAPTER 3
Scared to Play **22**

CHAPTER 4
A Secret Practice **30**

CHAPTER 5
Goal! **40**

JOSH CHAMPS

Soccer

AGE: 10
GRADE: 4
SUPER SPORTS ABILITY: Super skating

VICTORY
SCHOOL
SUPERSTARS

CARMEN   ALICIA   JOSH   DANNY   KENZIE   TYLER

VICTORY SCHOOL MAP

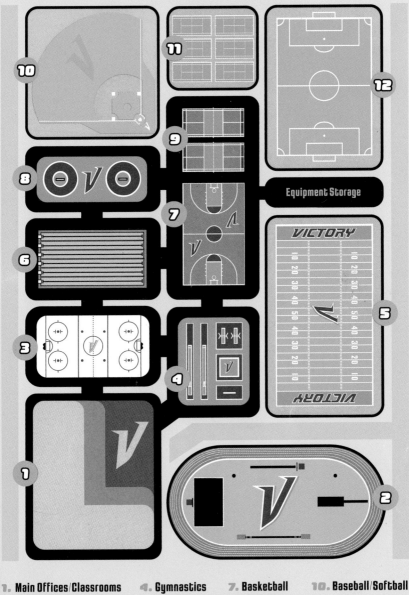

Equipment Storage

1. Main Offices/Classrooms
2. Track and Field
3. Hockey/Figure Skating
4. Gymnastics
5. Football
6. Swimming
7. Basketball
8. Wrestling
9. Volleyball
10. Baseball/Softball
11. Tennis
12. Soccer

Spring Break

I sit in the classroom and stare at the clock. I think the teacher is talking about the life cycle of frogs, but I'm not really listening.

I look over at my friends, Carmen and Brendan, sitting next to me. They are not listening either. We all have our eyes glued to the clock. It reads 2:57.

When the clock hits three, our science class will be over and vacation will begin.

Today is the last day of school before spring break at Victory School for Super Athletes. None of us can wait to get a week off from class.

No homework. No studying. And no lectures about frogs. We can spend the entire week just playing sports.

All of us who go to Victory are amazing athletes. We are all stars at one sport or another.

Carmen plays basketball. She is the best player I have ever seen. She can dribble so fast that the ball is just a blur.

As for Brendan and me? We play hockey. Brendan shoots the hardest slap shot on the team, while my super skating makes me impossible to stop.

Ring! The bell goes off, signaling the end of class. The students stand up and cheer.

As we walk out of the classroom, Carmen says, "Josh, a bunch of us are going to the field to play soccer after school. You should come, too."

"Soccer?" I say. "No thanks. We're going to the rink to play hockey, right, Brendan?"

"Well," says Brendan, "I think it might be fun to take a break from hockey for the day."

I scratch my head. "But I really need to work on my skating moves and get better at hockey," I say. "I don't know anything about soccer."

"Neither do I," says Brendan. "That's why it would be fun to try it."

"Yeah," says Carmen. "This week is our one chance to take a break from our regular sports and just play something for the fun of it. Now that it's basketball season, I miss playing soccer."

"I don't really want to play. I mean, who wants to play just for kicks?" I say. "I was planning on using the week to get better at hockey."

"Okay, suit yourself," says Carmen.

So I walk to the rink alone.

I spend an hour at the hockey rink by myself. It's fun to practice my skating, but it is also a little lonely. Maybe I should have played soccer instead.

The next morning, Brendan and I walk past the soccer field on our way to the ice rink. We are planning to play hockey.

Carmen and a group of other kids are at the field. Carmen jogs over to us.

"You guys should play," she says. "We are just about to start a game."

"We're going to the rink," I say.

Brendan looks at me. "Well," he says, "I would really like to play soccer."

"Again?" I ask. This time I am a little angry.

"We can still play hockey," he says. "We can play after the soccer game."

"Come on," says Carmen. "You will love it. Trust me."

I guess Brendan is right. There is no rush to get to the rink. We have all day to play hockey.

"Okay," I say and smile. "I'll play. Just let me change."

"Yes!" say Carmen and Brendan.

As the game begins, I immediately try to use my super skating footwork to dribble the soccer ball. It does not work. I trip and land flat on my back.

The next time the ball is near me, I again try to use my quick feet just like I would on the ice. But my legs get tangled, and I end up on the ground again. This is no fun at all.

Finally, I try one last time. I race toward the ball, stop it with my feet, then try to kick it to a teammate. But I completely miss the ball. And yes, I end up on the grass again. The players all sprint past me. Some of them laugh.

When no one is looking, I leave the field, grab my hockey bag, and take off for the rink. I have had enough. Soccer is just not my sport.

At the hockey rink, I am alone again. I skate back and forth across the ice, practicing my quick stops. I have gotten a lot better since I first went out for hockey. See? It pays to practice!

Suddenly I hear my name. I turn around. Standing behind the hockey boards is Carmen.

I skate over to her. "Hi, Carmen," I say.

"Why did you leave the soccer game, Josh?" Carmen asks.

"I just didn't feel like playing," I say. "I wasn't having any fun."

"Why? Because you were having a hard time with it?" asks Carmen.

"Of course," I say. I am getting a little angry at her. I wish Carmen would quit bugging me about soccer. "I guess I felt kind of dumb. I couldn't do anything."

"You know, Josh," says Carmen, "I wasn't very good at soccer when I first tried playing either. But I practiced, and I got better."

"But I'm not interested in becoming a good soccer player," I say. "I like being on ice." I show her a little fancy skating to prove my point.

"I know you do. But I don't think that's why you don't want to play," she says.

"What are you talking about?" I ask.

"I think you're afraid of looking silly, and you're afraid of being unsure of yourself," says Carmen. "That's okay. Trying a new sport can be a little scary."

"I'm not afraid," I say. "Remember, I wasn't good at hockey when I first started. But I wasn't afraid to play it."

"That's true," says Carmen. "But you were already a super skater."

"Why do you care so much, anyway?" I say.

"Because I think if you give soccer a try, you'd really like it." Carmen looks at the clock.

"I have to go," she says. "Tomorrow I'll be at the soccer field at eight in the morning. Stop by, and I'll help you learn how to play."

"I'll think about it," I say.

Carmen leaves. The rink is dead silent. I wonder if maybe Carmen's right. Maybe I am afraid to play soccer.

In bed that night, I think about what Carmen said. I can barely sleep. But when morning finally comes, my mind is made up. I'm going to give soccer another try.

I meet Carmen at the field at eight o'clock.

"I'm really glad you came, Josh," she says. Carmen kicks me a ball.

"Just dribble it to the center line and back," she adds.

I begin dribbling the ball. I move my feet quickly, like I'm on the ice. But immediately my legs get twisted up, and I fall to the grass.

Carmen laughs.

"It's not funny," I say.

"It's a little funny," she says. "Try it again."

So I hop up and try to use my super footwork again. Just when I think I am about to learn how to do it, my feet slam together and I crash to the ground.

Carmen laughs again.

"It's not funny, Carmen," I say. But this time I can't help laughing.

"See, it *is* funny, isn't it?" she says.

"Maybe a little," I say with a smile. "But can you teach me so I don't fall down all the time?"

"I think I know your problem," says Carmen.

"What is it?" I ask.

"You're trying to use your super skating moves on the soccer field," she says. "You have to forget about hockey and just try to run like a normal kid."

"I'll try," I say.

It works. Instead of moving my feet quickly, I slow down and just let my feet glide across the soccer field.

"You're doing it!" yells Carmen.

Before you know it, I have dribbled the ball to the center line. I turn around and dribble back. I don't fall down once.

"You were right. This is fun," I say.

"I told you so," says Carmen.

We spend the next two hours dribbling and kicking the soccer ball all over the field. I am still not a great player. But I have gotten *much* better. And I am having a good time playing a sport just for the fun of it.

"Hey, Josh," says Carmen. "I have an idea."

"What?" I ask.

"It's almost ten o'clock. The other kids are going to be here soon. You should go hide in the trees over there."

"Why?" I ask.

"After everyone else gets here, you can sneak out and pretend that you just arrived," she says. "When you start playing and everyone sees how good you are, we can have a fun joke and pretend that you suddenly just got better."

"I like it," I say. I run to the pine trees near the field and wait for our other friends to show up.

Just like Carmen and I planned, I sneak up to the field after the other kids have gotten there.

"Hi, Josh!" shouts Carmen. She pretends she hasn't seen me all morning.

"Hi," I say.

"You should play with us," she says.

"No thanks," I say, trying not to smile. "I don't like soccer."

"Come on, Josh," says Brendan. "Stay and play."

I pause. I am trying to be dramatic. "Okay, I suppose," I say. "But you know I'm not very good." Carmen and I share a secret smile.

The game begins. Carmen and I are on the same team. Brendan is on the other team.

I stay back for a few minutes and let the other kids go after the ball.

I wait for my perfect chance, and then I pounce.

I control the ball with my feet and begin to dribble it quickly up the sideline. When Brendan comes over to stop me, I kick the ball hard toward Carmen.

She dances around a defender, dribbles toward the goal, and fires a hard shot at the net. The goalie dives for the ball but cannot stop it. Goal!

Carmen rushes over to me and we celebrate.

"How did you do that?" asks Brendan. "I didn't think you could play soccer."

"I don't know," I say. "I guess I just learned. It's kind of wild!"

Carmen and I share a big laugh.

"What's going on?" Brendan asks.

"Should we tell him?" I ask.

"I suppose," says Carmen.

"Carmen and I have been here for more than two hours," I say. "She taught me how to play."

"So you have been practicing all morning?" asks Brendan. "You were joking about not liking soccer?"

"Good one, huh?" I say with a grin.

"Let's play the game," says Brendan. He laughs and grabs the ball from Carmen.

We finish the first game, then play two more games after that. I never get tired.

I have a blast. I don't score any goals, and I still trip over my own feet a couple of times. But I have a great time.

I think this week I'm going to take a short break from hockey. This week I'm going to play a sport just for the fun of it. I'm going to play soccer, and I'm going to play it just for kicks.

GLOSSARY

amazing (uh-MAZE-ing)—causing great wonder or surprise

athletes (ATH-leets)—people who play sports

defender (di-FEN-der)—a player who tries to stop the other team from scoring points

dramatic (druh-MAT-ik)—making a big fuss about something

dribble (DRIB-uhl)—in basketball, to bounce the ball while running and keeping it under control; in soccer, to move the ball with gentle kicks while running.

immediately (i-MEE-dee-it-lee)—now or at once

sideline (SIDE-line)—a line that marks the side boundary of the playing area in sports such as soccer

signaling (SIG-nuhl-ing)—sending a message

SOCCER IN HISTORY

 1500 B.C.
The earliest known version of soccer is played in China.

 1862 A.D.
The first organized soccer club in the United States is formed in Boston. The team is called the Oneidas.

 1885
The United States plays Canada for the first time. This is the first international game to be played outside the British Isles.

 1930
The first World Cup is played in **Uruguay**.

 1975
Brazilian soccer star **Pelé** signs with the New York Cosmos for $4.5 million. He is one of the greatest players of all time.

 1996
Major League Soccer (MLS), the most popular U.S. soccer league, plays its first season.

 2006
Frenchman **Zinedine Zidane** is kicked out of the World Cup final after head butting Italy's Marco Materazzi.

 2007
British star **David Beckham** signs with the Los Angeles Galaxy, sparking a new interest in U.S. soccer.

 2010
In South Africa, **Spain** wins their first World Cup at Africa's first World Cup tournament.

VICTORY SCHOOL SUPERSTARS

Five Fouls and You're Out!

It's a Wrestling Mat, Not a Dance Floor

There's a Hurricane in the Pool!

There's No Crying in Baseball

Who Wants to Play Just for Kicks?

You Can't Spike Your Serves